OUTSIDE

WRITTEN AND ILLUSTRATED BY
PAULA KAREN DEWELL

Visit our website at www.StillwaterPress.com for more information.

First Stillwater River Publications Edition

Library of Congress Control Number 2019913489

ISBN-13: 978-1-950339-35-8
ISBN-10: 1-950339-35-1

12345678910

Written and illustrated by Paula Karen Dewell
Published by Stillwater River Publications, Pawtucket, RI 02860

The views and opinions expressed in this book are solely those of the author and do not necessarily reflect the views and opinions of the publisher.

DEDICATED
TO TOBIAS AND FRANCESCA

Outside

This was one of the little girl's first words. She thought that if she put on her yellow boots she could go outside. But sometimes it was raining or snowing too hard.

Still, she loved to be outside no matter the weather. The sun would always feel good as it warmed her. When the rain fell in a gentle sprinkle, she liked to feel it tickle her face. She could catch the warm drops on her tongue. Best of all there were puddles big and small. She would be the first to jump in, making big splashes.

When it was too rainy, the little girl would say, "Momma, make it stop raining!"

"I am not able to do that," her mother would say, "but remember that the rain gives drinks to the plants and animals. You can always look outside the window and see wonderful things."

As the weather turned cooler, the leaves of orange and yellow and red were such fun to play in.

THE WINTER SOMETIMES BROUGHT SNOWFLAKES. PRETTY CRYSTAL SHAPES WOULD SPIN DOWN AND MELT ON HER FACE AND TONGUE AS SHE LOOKED UP. THERE WERE SNOWMEN TO BUILD WITH CARROT NOSES, GLOSSY BLACK EYES, AND SMILING FACES.

THE CELEBRATION

TODAY WAS A SPECIAL DAY. THE LITTLE GIRL WAS CELEBRATING HER BIRTHDAY. FRIENDS AND FAMILY GATHERED, AS DID THE CHILDREN'S FAVORITE STUFFED ANIMAL FRIENDS. THERE WERE PRESENTS, CAKE, ALL KINDS OF FOOD, AND MOST OF ALL, LOTS OF LOVE.

THE GIRL'S GRANDMOTHER BROUGHT A GIFT WRAPPED IN BROWN PAPER AND DECORATED WITH LITTLE STARS AND TIED WITH A PURPLE BOW. ON THE PACKAGE THERE WAS A TAG THAT SAID, "OPEN THIS PRESENT LAST AND BE SURE TO SHARE IT WITH YOUR BROTHER!"

The children looked at the shape of the package.

"Is this a book?" they asked.

"Yes," said Grandma, "And it is very special."

"Why is it special?" asked the girl.

"Why? Why? Why?" asked her brother. (He liked to ask why about almost everything.)

"It is magical, and will take you to many places, near and far" said her grandmother.

As a very little girl, she loved books. Sometimes she would pretend to read to her brother. They thought that books were special in some ways and taught them many things. But real magic? That did not seem possible. As she looked across the room, she thought that she saw one of her stuffed animal friends wink!

Snow Snow Snow

It was a lovely party, but the children knew that this was certainly not an outside day. The air was filled with snow and the ground was covered with a white blanket. *I wish that it was summer*, thought the little girl. *Then we could go outside and run and play in the soft green fields. We could feel the warm sun and stay out late.*

But the snow kept falling and the wind was howling. The drifts were higher than the children's heads. The snow hung heavy on the branches of the trees. It was so cold that even the little bunnies were huddled together. Finally the wind stopped and the snow sparkled as it lay on the trees and streets. It was so pretty as the sky turned a beautiful deep blue and gradually melted into a dark night sky with twinkling stars. "Tomorrow you can play in the snow" said their parents.

"It's so hard to wait" answered the children.

"We know, but it is late" reminded their mother. "And you still have not opened one of your presents."

Bed Time Story

The children loved bedtime stories. They had almost forgotten about the gift that said, "Open me last!" The little boy picked up the present and said to his sister "Can we read this one?"

"Of course" Dad said. "As soon as you get ready for bed."

The children had such fun at the party, but they were tired after this busy day. Momma read the book to the children, and soon they were fast asleep. "Sweet dreams," said the parents as they turned off the lights.

The Balloons

It seemed like only moments before the children were awakened by light streaming through the windows. They were not prepared for what they saw was outside.

They saw very large balloons... waiting to take them away!
It would be fun to be on those seats, the girl thought. Without hesitating, she climbed aboard. Her brother usually did everything that she did, so he jumped on too.

The little girl wondered if her brother should come with her, but she also remembered that her grandmother said that she had to share the surprise.

"You have to hold on tightly," she said.

"I'm a big boy," he replied. "I can hold on, just like you."

THE CHILDREN QUICKLY FOUND THAT IT WAS EASY TO RIDE THE BALLOONS.
THEY ROSE HIGH INTO THE SKY. WARM AIR SURROUNDED THEM. THE HOUSES
BECAME SMALLER AND SMALLER AS THEY GLIDED BETWEEN THE FLUFFY CLOUDS.
"LOOK AT ALL THE OTHER BALLOONS!" THE LITTLE GIRL SAID TO HER BROTHER.
"THOSE CHILDREN MUST HAVE THE BOOK TOO."

SOON THEY CAME UPON A LARGE FIELD OF GRASS. THE BALLOONS
LANDED SLOWLY AND GENTLY. THERE WAS A BEAUTIFUL PATH FILLED
WITH ALL KINDS OF FLOWERS THAT LOOKED LIKE GIANTS WAVING IN THE BREEZE.

THE CHILDREN STEPPED ONTO THE PATH THAT LED THEM THROUGH THE FIELD. JUST AHEAD THEY SAW A VERY LARGE CAT. IT WAS BEAUTIFUL, WITH KIND GREEN EYES AND SOFT FLUFFY WHITE AND TAN FUR.

"WELCOME, I HAVE BEEN EXPECTING YOU. I'M MR. BENNY," SAID THE CAT.

ANIMALS CAN'T TALK, THOUGHT THE LITTLE GIRL, AS SHE SAW TWO LITTLE KITTENS PEEK OUT FROM BEHIND THE GRASS.

"I HAVE TO TAKE CARE OF MY LITTLE ONES NOW, BUT I WILL SEE YOU LATER," SAID MR. BENNY. "JUST FOLLOW THE PATH AND THE GEESE WILL SHOW YOU THE WAY."

"ARE THERE MONSTERS HERE?" ASKED THE LITTLE BOY.

"OH NO," SAID THE CAT. "WELL, THERE ARE FRIENDLY MONSTERS I SUPPOSE. THEY WILL HELP YOU FIND YOUR WAY BACK TO THE TRAILS IF YOU GET LOST. PLEASE DO NOT BE SCARED. THIS IS A VERY SAFE PLACE FOR ALL CREATURES."

The Geese

So the children set out on their way down the path where the geese were waiting. They had orange beaks and white downy feathers. They seemed to be talking to each other.

This is a very unusual outside place, thought the girl. "We have to take care of our goslings now" the geese told them, "but if you continue along this way you will see many baby animals."

The Birds

"Look, there are birds!" the little girl said to her brother. "They have just finished building their nest." The children quietly peeked into the nest, where they saw fragile eggs nestled into a soft bed of grass and twigs.

Little Sparrows

There were birds everywhere, and many other nests among the trees. Soon there would be little ones poking out of their shells. They would be very hungry and the big birds would have to bring them many yummy worms until they were strong enough to fly away.

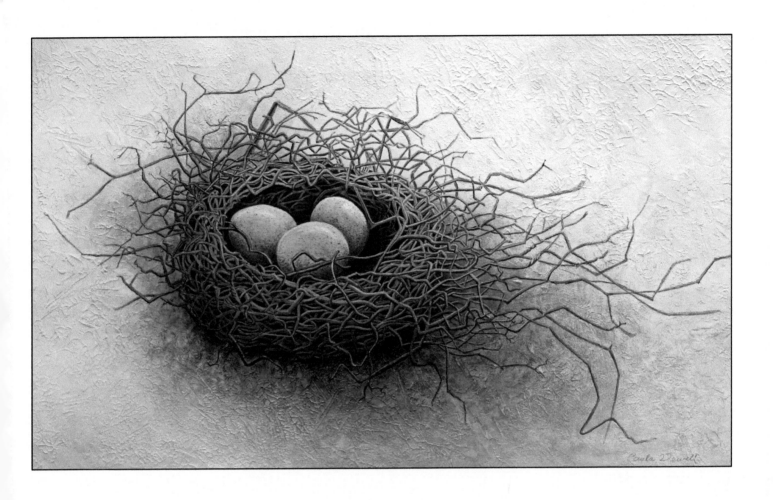

As they walked along the path, they saw some eggs that had begun to hatch. The little chicks were making peeping sounds. The children watched as they poked out of their shells. They had fuzzy yellow fur that would soon turn into feathers, and wobbly legs that would soon be strong.

Field of Flowers

As the girl and her brother walked along, they came upon a field filled with giant sunflowers. They were dipping and swaying in the wind, and seemed to be looking down and saying "thank you" to another child who had just finished watering. *We all have to help to take care of this beautiful place,* thought the little girl.

Then they saw another child blowing on a giant dandelion. The fluffy seeds began to glitter as they scattered.

The butterflies glided through the air above. Like so many other things they had seen, these were not ordinary butterflies. They were humming as they spread their giant wings and swooped down to play tag with the children.

Leap Frog

The girl and boy followed the butterflies to a pond with glistening frogs of many colors. "Will you play leap frog with us? Please?" asked the frogs. By now the children were used to the different creatures talking to them. They were such happy frogs and the children wanted to stay, but there were more things to see and do. The leaping frogs led the children through a corn maze.

The Sea Shore

At the clearing beyond the maze, they glimpsed the sea. The children loved to play in the waves and the sand so they walked down to the shore. The little girl wrote the words "I Love You" in the sand. The waves came in and the waves went out, but the words remained carved in the sand. "How can this happen?" she wondered aloud. Just then Mr. Benny reappeared. He said, "Love is something that never ends, this is why the waves cannot erase the feelings that you have written in sand... not in this place. It is getting late. Come with me... I have planned something special."

THE SURPRISE

AS THEY FOLLOWED MR. BENNY THE CHILDREN LOOKED BACK
AT THE SEA AND SAW THE MOON RISING IN THE SKY, SHINING
ITS LIGHT THROUGH THE HAZE AND IRIDESCENT ON THE WATER.

SOON THEY SAW THE SURPRISE. WAITING FOR THEM WERE THEIR
FAVORITE STUFFED ANIMALS AND A SPLENDID TEA PARTY PICNIC
SHOWERED IN THE LIGHT OF THE RISING FULL MOON.

SUDDENLY THEY REMEMBERED HOW HUNGRY THEY WERE. MR. RABBIT
WAS THERE TO HELP SERVE. THERE WAS FRUIT AND CHEESE
AND CAKE AND OTHER DELICIOUS FOOD UNDER THE SHIMMERING LIGHTS.

JUST THEN THEY SAW A LITTLE MOUSE.

"OH NO!"

"MR. BENNY... STOP THAT MOUSE!

HE IS RUNNING AWAY WITH SOME OF THE CHEESE!"

The mouse looked so sad when he heard the little girl. But Mr. Benny was not your usual cat. "Everyone gets hungry and there is plenty of cheese to share with those who live and work here. Everyone here takes care of each other." The children began to realize that this was a very wise cat.

The Journey Home

This was such a perfect ending to their adventure. "Thank you so much," said the little girl as her brother nodded.

Mr. Benny smiled at the children as they gathered and said goodbye to each other. They missed their families but were sad to be leaving. There were so many magical places still left to explore. Mr. Benny said, "I know it is hard to leave, but you can always return. Can you tell me what you have learned from this adventure?" The children paused and thought for a minute.

"I LEARNED THAT WE HAVE TO TAKE CARE OF THE LAND AND EVERYTHING

THAT LIVES HERE... EVEN THE MOUSE," SAID THE LITTLE GIRL.

"YES," SAID MR. BENNY "BUT WHEN YOU GET BACK TO YOUR HOME, YOU

WILL ALSO SEE MANY BEAUTIFUL THINGS AND PLACES ALL AROUND YOU.

REMEMBER HOW SPECIAL THE EARTH IS AND THAT WE HAVE TO TAKE

CARE OF IT. MOST IMPORTANTLY, YOU NEED TO LOVE AND CARE FOR

EACH OTHER."

THE GIRL PUT HER ARM AROUND HER LITTLE BROTHER.

EPILOGUE

DREAMS CAN BE DIFFERENT FOR EVERYONE.

WHERE WOULD YOU LIKE THE BALLOONS TO TAKE YOU?

About The Author

Paula Karen Dewell is a regional artist who lives along the south coast of Rhode Island with her husband Glenn. She is an elected artist member of the Art League of Rhode Island and the Lyme Art Association. Her artwork has been exhibited in galleries in Rhode Island, Connecticut and Massachusetts, and can be found in private collections in the United States and Great Britain.

Paula is a retired high school art educator who continues her teaching as adjunct faculty at Rhode Island School of Design. Being an educator has allowed Paula to enjoy working in a variety of media. Her subject matter ranges from portraits to landscapes to wildlife to still life and floral paintings. She loves it all!

CPSIA information can be obtained
at www.ICGtesting.com
Printed in the USA
BVHW021338101019
560708BV00001B/5/P